SUPERGIRL TAKES OFF!

by Courtney Carbone

illustrated by Erik Doescher

Random House 🏠 New York

Meet Supergirl!
Her real name
is Kara Zor-El.
She is a super hero!

Supergirl grew up
on a planet far,
far from Earth.

But her planet

was not stable.

It was about to explode!

Supergirl's family
wanted to keep
her safe.

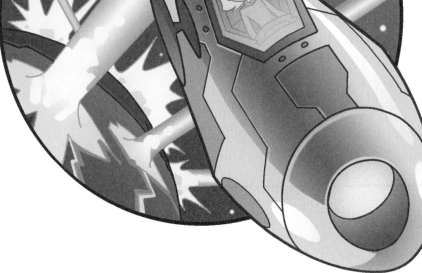

They sent her
to live on Earth
with her cousin,
Superman!

Superman was happy
to see Supergirl.
He showed her
around Metropolis,
the city he called home.

As she got older,
Supergirl's powers
began to grow.
She had super-strength,

super-speed,

and X-ray vision!

Supergirl's heat vision
can melt anything.

Her super-breath can
blow the villains away!

Being a super hero
is fun and exciting.
No job is too big
for Supergirl.

Her Super-Cat,
Streaky,
has powers, too!

Supergirl joins
the Super Friends
to stop villains
like Poison Ivy.

Supergirl has to be
on the lookout
for danger.

Bad guys are always threatening Earth.

Fighting crime is
a full-time job!
Supergirl is up
for the challenge.

Supergirl takes off.

She will save the day!